for Thalia and Roland
M·E·

for Jean and Caroline
G·R·

Published in 1994 by Magi Publications
in association with Star Books International, 55 Crowland Avenue, Hayes, Middx UB3 4JP

Text © 1994 by Mark Ezra
Illustrations © 1994 by Gavin Rowe

Printed and bound in Belgium by Proost N.V.Turnhout

ISBN 1 85430 259 0

MARK EZRA

The Sleepy Dormouse

pictures by GAVIN ROWE

Magi Publications, London

The sleepy dormouse was small and round, and he slept with his little tail tucked up over his head. Every now and then he would give a little sigh or a little snore, but he would not wake up.

One day, when the first blossom was on the trees, the harvest mice came round. "Get up, Dormouse!" they called. "Spring has arrived!" The sleepy dormouse simply rolled over and went back to sleep.

The next morning Scraggly Sam came rooting around, looking for something to eat. Perhaps a clutch of eggs? Or a fat little hedgehog or two? *They* would be delicious in a stew.

As he padded along the hedgerow, something fell out.
It was a little nest made of woven grass.
Inside Scraggly Sam found the sleepy dormouse.
"Aha!" he said. "Lunch!"
He poked the furry little body.
"Hm," he said. "Not much meat on this one!"

Scraggly Sam took the sleepy dormouse home,
put him under a heavy flowerpot and gave him a
little water. Then he dropped some sunflower seeds
and a handful of hazelnuts through the hole at the top.
The sleepy dormouse woke up. He saw the seeds
and the nuts.
"This is the life!" he said, eating them all up.
Then he went back to sleep.

A few days later the dormouse heard a scratching.
"Go away, I'm sleeping," he mumbled.
"It's us, the harvest mice," said a voice from outside.
"You've got to wake up. You're in terrible danger!"

"Nonsense!" replied the sleepy dormouse. "Someone's looking after me. I get food every day."
"That's because Scraggly Sam is fattening you up," cried the harvest mice. "We've been watching him!"

The harvest mice tried to pull the poor little dormouse out through the hole in the flowerpot, but he was already much too fat. He squeaked so loudly that Scraggly Sam came to see what all the noise was about. The harvest mice ran off and hid in the long grass.

Scraggly Sam prodded the little dormouse
through the hole.
"Good," he said. "You're much plumper
already. Soon you'll be fat enough to eat.
I'll have you for supper on Sunday."

The dormouse was wide awake now.
His eyes were round with fear, and
he trembled for his life.
He heard the scratching
sound again.

"It's us, we're back!" called the harvest mice.
"Now listen, we've got a plan . . . ."

The next day the dormouse didn't gobble up all
his food. He ate only the nuts. Then he buried the
sunflower seeds in a hole and sprinkled them with
his daily ration of water.

On Monday the sunflower seeds
started to sprout.

On Tuesday they were already higher
than he was.

By the end of the week they had almost
filled the flowerpot.

On Sunday the sunflower seedlings forced their way up through the hole in the top, and the bottom of the pot began to lift off the ground.

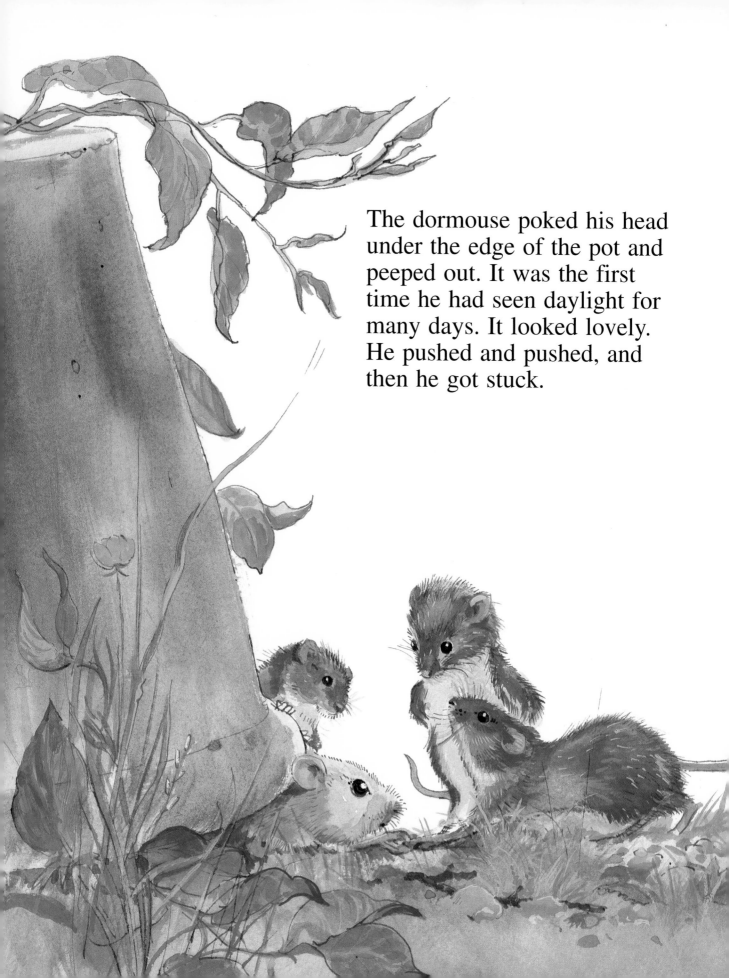

The dormouse poked his head under the edge of the pot and peeped out. It was the first time he had seen daylight for many days. It looked lovely. He pushed and pushed, and then he got stuck.

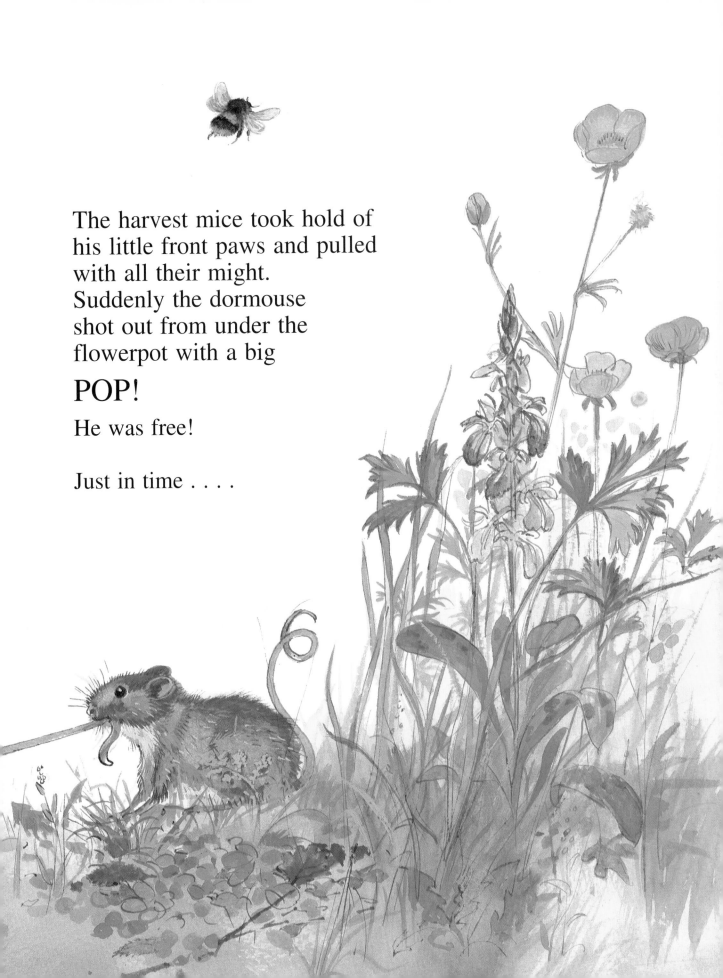

The harvest mice took hold of
his little front paws and pulled
with all their might.
Suddenly the dormouse
shot out from under the
flowerpot with a big

POP!

He was free!

Just in time . . . .

Scraggly Sam was coming along, licking his
lips hungrily. But when he lifted up the pot he found
just a thick tangle of sunflowers, pointing to the sun!
He had an apple for his supper and went to bed in a
very bad temper.

"Thank you for saving my life", said the dormouse that night, as the harvest mice tucked him up in one of their spare nests. And then before you could say "sunflower seeds", he'd curled his tail up over his head and gone to sleep!